OH NO, BOBO!
Donna David
Laura Watkins
QED

Everyone in the jungle was fast asleep.
Everyone except for Bobo.

His branch
was too hard!

The bark was
too scratchy!

And a knobbly bit was
digging in his ear!

This book belongs to:

....

....

For Sofia, Evie
and Louis - DD

For Danielle, Ioana,
Sof, Pants, Bex and
Richard - LW

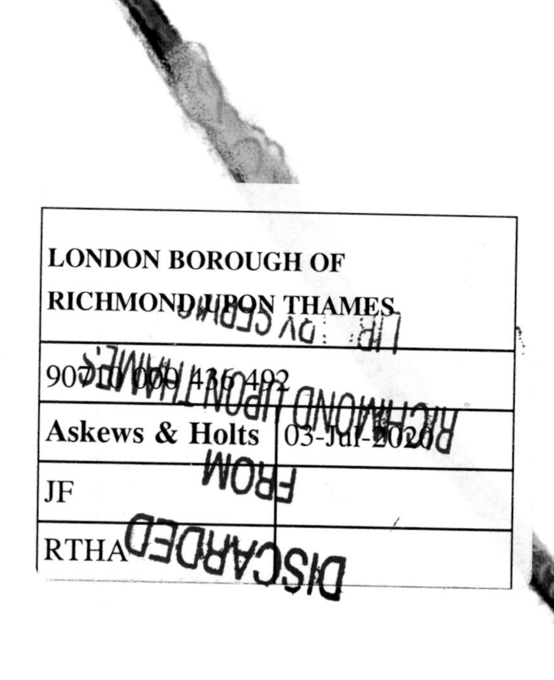

Quarto is the authority on a wide range of topics.
Quarto educates, entertains and enriches the lives of our readers—enthusiasts and lovers of hands-on living.
www.quartoknows.com

Author: Donna David
Illustrator: Laura Watkins
Designer: Victoria Kimonidou
Editor: Ellie Brough

This edition first published in 2020 by QED Publishing,
an imprint of The Quarto Group.
The Old Brewery, 6 Blundell Street,
London N7 9BH, United Kingdom.
T (0)20 7700 6700 F (0)20 7700 8066
www.QuartoKnows.com

A catalogue record for this book is available from the British Library.

ISBN 978 0 7112 5109 0

Manufactured in Guangdong,China TT012020

9 8 7 6 5 4 3 2 1

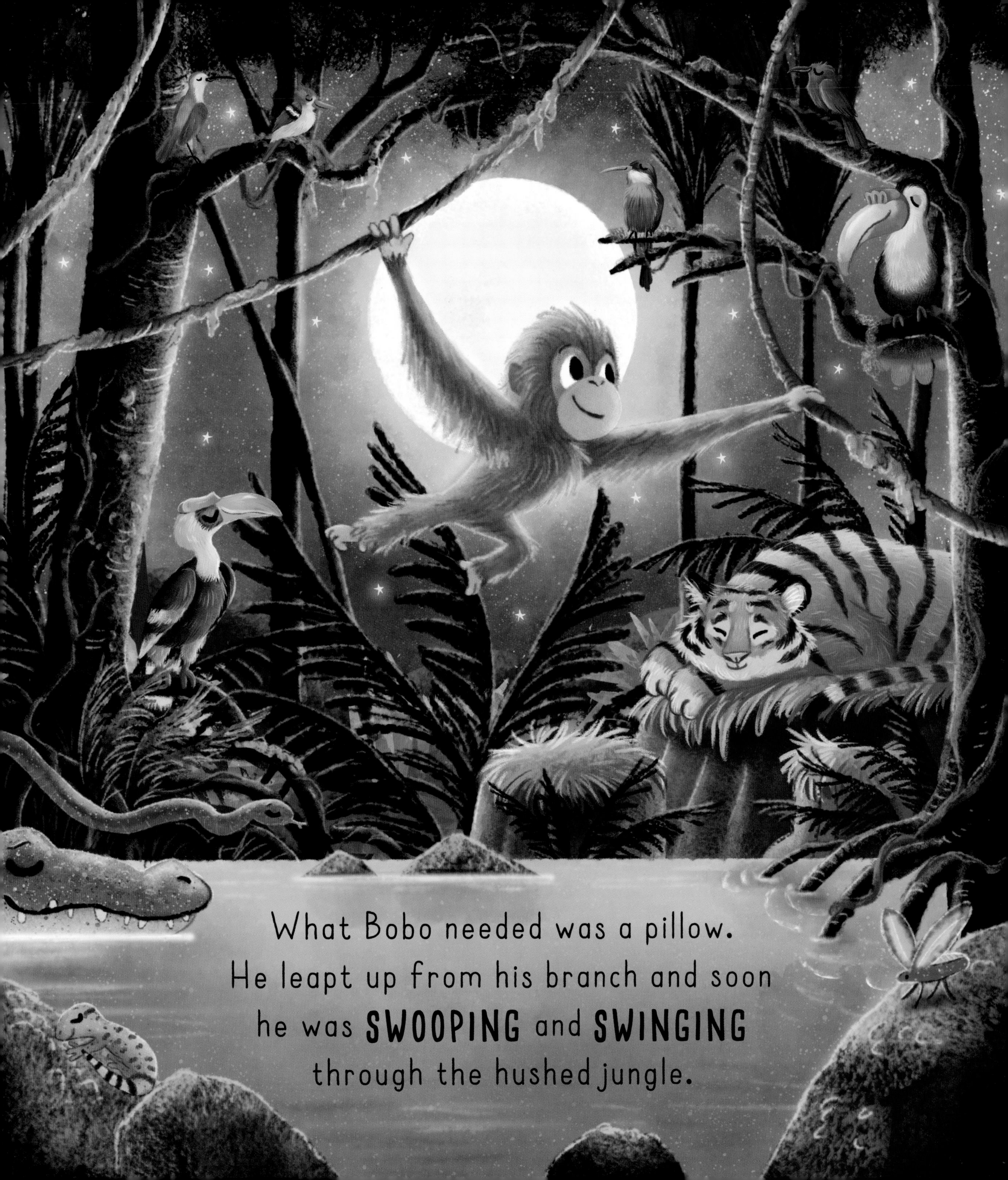

What Bobo needed was a pillow.
He leapt up from his branch and soon
he was **SWOOPING** and **SWINGING**
through the hushed jungle.

A flash of red caught his eye. Bobo stopped and stared at the sleeping parrots. He reached out to stroke their soft feathers.

But Bobo really needed
a pillow! So, very gently,
he pulled out one of
Troy's feathers...

"SQUAWK!"

Troy flapped his wings angrily.
Parrots were too noisy to make a
perfect pillow! Bobo swung away...

Until he heard a rustling noise below.
It was Lulu the slow loris!
She looked so warm and oh, so cuddly.
Bobo reached out his hand...

"Oh no... Bobo!
Please... don't... stroke...
me..." said Lulu.

But Lulu looked so comfortable.
Bobo very gently laid his head on her.

PERFECT!

But Lulu slowly turned her head and...

"YEOUCH!" screamed Bobo.

Slow lorises were too bite-y to make a perfect pillow!

He raced through the jungle again and almost crashed into a nest of giant squirrels. He reached out and tickled a silky-smooth tail...

"Oh no, Bobo. Please don't touch my tail!" cried Sami the Squirrel.

But Bobo didn't listen. He scooped Sami up in his arms and pulled out a tuft of hair. Sami was not happy. He lifted his tail, aimed his bottom and...

PARRRR

Bobo dropped Sami in horror.
Squirrels were too stinky to make the perfect pillow!

Tired and grumpy, Bobo trudged through the jungle. How was he ever going to sleep now?

Then everything started to shake.
A low rumbling came through the trees.

"I CAN'T SLEEP!"
came a thundering voice.
"I NEED A PILLOW!"

"ME TOO!" cried Bobo. He leapt through the bushes and found a herd of sleeping elephants.

Except for Elsie,
who was still awake...

"Orangutan!" giggled Elsie,
"You're so soft and velvety!"

"Oh no," said Bobo.

Elsie stroked Bobo.
"You're so bushy
and silky-smooth."

"OH, NO NO!"
shouted Bobo.

She wrapped him up
in her trunk. "You're
so warm and cuddly."

"AGGGHHHHHHH!"
bellowed Bobo.

He launched himself out
of Elsie's trunk and...

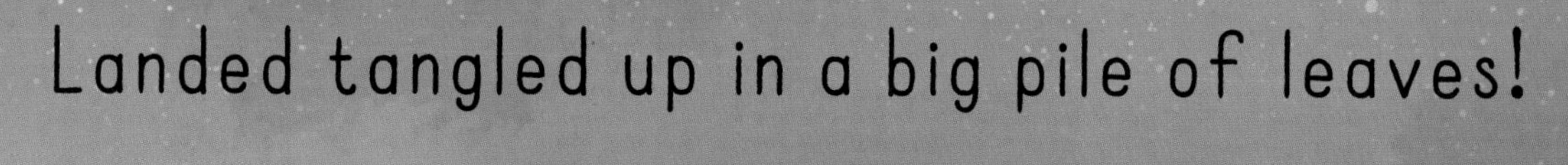

Landed tangled up in a big pile of leaves!

"I WANT MY MUMMY!" cried Bobo.

Elsie reached out to pick Bobo up just as her dad woke up. "No, no Elsie," he said.

"You know the rules; you have to ask.
Bobo, may I help you clean up?" he asked, kindly.

"Can I help too?" Elsie asked, sheepishly.
Bobo nodded again.

"I'm sorry," Elsie whispered.
Bobo felt sorry too. He'd forgotten to ask as well.

When Bobo was clean, he trudged back to his mum. She looked so warm and cuddly and soft.

Bobo had an important question to ask.

"Can I have a cuddle please?" he asked.

Mum nodded sleepily and Bobo crawled into her arms. He'd found the **PERFECT PILLOW** after all.

NEXT STEPS

Discussion and comprehension

Discuss the story with the children and ask the following questions, encouraging them to take turns and give full answers if they can. Offer support by turning to the appropriate pages of the book if needed.

- What happened when Bobo didn't listen to the parrot?
- How does the author show us in the text that the animals are annoyed?
- Can you think of a time when you haven't listened when someone asked you not to do something?
- Where did Bobo find his perfect pillow at the end of the story?
- What lesson do you think Bobo learned?

Animal description

Give each child a piece of paper divided into four marked boxes with a circle in the middle. Ask them to draw a picture of their favourite animal from the book in the circle and write the animal's name underneath. Reinforce some of the phrases that the author uses to describe the animals, for example 'bushy and silky smooth' or 'warm and oh, so cuddly'. Label the four boxes: what does this animal look like? Where does this animal live? What noise does this animal make when they are cross? What do you know about this animal? Encourage and support the children to write a sentence under the heading in each box using the book to help them. When the children have finished, encourage them to share their animal descriptions with each other.

Paper bag Bobo puppet

Give each child a small paper plate and some thick orange wax crayons. Ask them to lightly colour the plate orange and to draw Bobo's face on the plate. Give them two small googly eyes to stick on. Give them some orange coloured card to cut out two arms and two ears. Stick the ears onto the plate. Then give each child a brown paper bag and help them to staple the arms and the plate to the paper bag. Encourage the children to retell the story with their own Bobo puppet!